MW01065602

Arizona
Wildflowers

A children's
field guide to
the state's most
common flowers

Interpreting the Great Outdoors

Text by Beverly Magley, Illustrations by DD Dowden

For Barbara & Jack,
Tom and Michael—
who taught me new
ways to see Arizona

Mags

Interpreting the Great Outdoors

Nature's wonders, such as the wildflowers, are certainly remarkable, but unfortunately many people—especially young people—know little about them. That's one reason Falcon Press has launched this series of books called Interpreting the Great Outdoors.

Other books in the series include *The Tree Giants: The Story of the Redwoods, the World's Largest Trees; The Fire Mountains: The Story of the Cascade Volcanoes;* and *California Wildflowers.*

To get extra copies of this book or others in the Interpreting the Great Outdoors series, write to Falcon Press, P.O. Box 1718, Helena, MT 59624. Or call toll-free 1-800-582-2665. Falcon Press publishes and distributes a wide variety of books and calendars, so be sure to ask for our free catalog.

Copyright © 1991
by Falcon Press Publishing Co., Inc.,
Billings and Helena, Montana.

All rights reserved, including the right to reproduce any part of this book in any form, with the exception of brief quotations included in a review, without the written permission of the publisher.

Botanical consultant—Janice Emily Bowers

Design, illustrations, editing, typesetting, and other prepress work by Falcon Press, Helena, Montana. Printed in Hong Kong.

Library of Congress Number 91-58054
ISBN 1-56044-096-1

Contents

Introduction

A single white blossom hangs from a crack in a cliff.
Tiny yellow blooms cling to a mountain peak.
A starburst of magenta petals crowns a cactus.
Tall blue flowers sway in the shade of a forest.

Arizona is incredibly diverse—from flat sandy deserts to
mountain peaks, from steep-walled canyons to densely forested
plateaus. And like the terrain, the plant life is varied, too. About
3,800 species call Arizona home.

Flowering plants are a recent arrival to our world, if you
consider 120 million years recent. (Travel to the bottom of the
Grand Canyon and view rocks two billion years old, and flowers
begin to seem pretty new.) Flowering plants are unique because
each of their seeds has a protective, nourishing shell that gives
the seed a better chance of survival.

Flower blossoms entice visitors with their nectar, and the
nectar-eaters then pollinate the blossoms so they can produce
seeds. A nice trade! So when you see an ant crawling inside a
flower or watch a hummingbird sipping nectar, remember they
are essential to the survival of flowers. In addition to providing
food, flowers also provide shelter for insects and other tiny
critters.

Humans are dependent on flowering plants. We eat them, and
make medicines, oils, perfumes, and dyes from them. Many
flowers are grown just so we can use them. But wildflowers are
special. It is enough simply to love their beauty. Most flowers
don't mind if you touch them very gently or lean down for a
whiff of their lovely fragrance. Perhaps they even hope you'll
appreciate their beautiful colors and shapes.

But remember, if you pick a flower it dies. When you leave it
blooming in its home, the blossom will eventually fade but its
seeds will scatter and provide another year of beautiful
wildflowers that you can come back to enjoy.

To see a world in a grain of sand,
And heaven in a wild flower,
Hold infinity in the palm of your hand
And eternity in an hour.

William Blake

Woodlands

Oaks, junipers, and pinyon pines characterize this semi-arid life zone. Most wildflowers here are perennials—that is, they survive from one year to the next. Many blossom twice a year in response to moisture, in springtime, and again after the late summer rains have soaked the ground. Pinyon jays, bushy-tailed wood rats, and gray warblers live here.

Buffalo Gourd

other names: Coyote Melon, Chili Coyote, Calabazilla
height: up to 1', with stems up to 20' long
season: April to October

Yellow blossoms often hide under the hairy, triangular leaves, but the awful-tasting fruits, or gourds, are easy to see in winter when the leaves have died. Coyotes eat the gourds, and people dry and paint them for house ornaments. Early settlers crushed the roots of the plant to make soap.

Sacred Datura

other names: Jimsonweed, Moon Lily, Thorn Apple
height: up to 3'
season: May to October

Sit by a datura plant some evening and watch the flower buds slowly unfurl into trumpet-shaped blossoms. The puff of fragrance from each bloom must be the sweetest aroma in the entire world. Sacred datura has big, coarse, gray-green leaves that don't smell very nice, and a prickly round fruit. Don't eat any parts of this plant—even though it's related to the potato, it is quite poisonous.

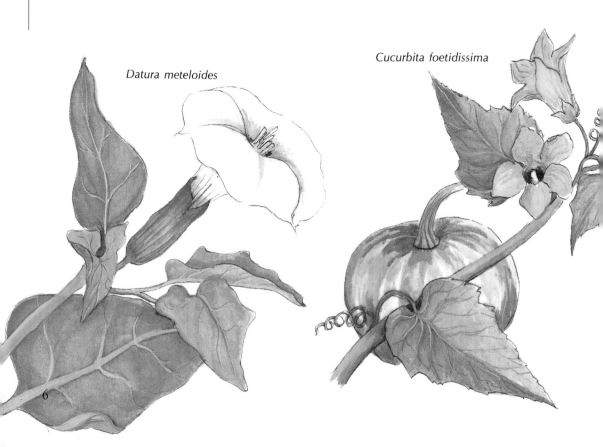

Datura meteloides

Cucurbita foetidissima

Prickly Poppy

other names: Thistle Poppy, Cowboy's Fried Egg, Chicalote
height: 3' to 4'
season: March to October

The tissue-thin petals and yellow centers look a bit like a fried egg. But don't eat it! The prickly, poisonous stems, leaves, and seedpods are avoided by livestock. The sap is useful to humans, though, for medicinal purposes.

Horsemint

other names: Lemon Mint, Wild Bergamot
height: 1' to 3'
season: June to August

Gently feel the stem of this plant—mints have square stems. The leaves can be used to make tea. Wild animals and cattle like horsemint, but horses don't. Maybe we should change the name to deermint?

Prince's Plume

other names: Desert Plume, Golden Prince's Plume
height: 18" to 5'
season: April to September

Like feathers in a cap, Prince's plume waves high above the woodland floor. Blossoming begins at the top of the stalk, and by the time the lower parts are in bloom, the top has already formed seedpods. The plant gets its yellow color from selenium, a mineral poisonous to mammals.

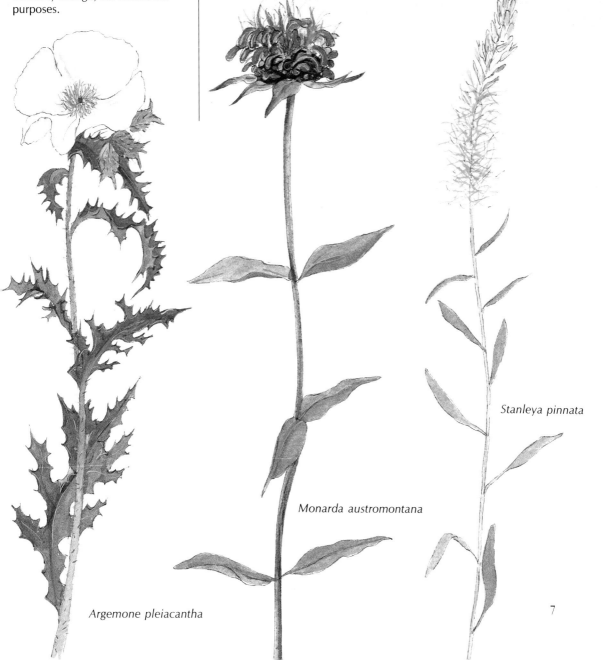

Argemone pleiacantha

Monarda austromontana

Stanleya pinnata

Blanketflower

other names: Firewheel, Indian Blanket
height: 12" to 18"
season: April to September

This flower's name is easy to remember because its blossoms can blanket a field in showy, bright colors. Individually, each flower looks like a fiery pinwheel. Look closely at the blossom. It is called a composite because the brightly-colored pinwheel parts are rays and the center cone is composed of dozens of tightly packed individual flowers.

Beardtongue

other names: Golden-beard Penstemon
height: 15" to 4'
season: May to August

Such a funny-faced flower! A beard of long yellowish hairs dangles from the lower lip of each tubular blossom, while the upper lip has what looks like two tiny teeth projecting forward. Hummingbirds and insects with long mouth parts love to feed on the sweet nectar secreted deep inside the flower.

Blue Flax

other names: Prairie Flax, Lewis' Flax
height: 6" to 18"
season: April to September

Delicate sky-blue flowers sway gently on a slender stem. Humans know the long, tough fibers in the stem are very useful. Long ago, Egyptians wrapped their mummies in cloth woven from flax, early Indians used the fibers to make ropes and fishing lines, and today, a relative of blue flax is cultivated to make linen fabric and linseed oil.

Linum perenne var. lewisii

Penstemon barbatus

Gaillardia pulchella

Mariposa

other names: none
height: 6" to 18"
season: April to June

Early explorers thought this blossom looked like a butterfly, called "mariposa" in Spanish. Calochortus is the Greek word for "beautiful grass." You'll probably agree that this is like a beautiful butterfly adorning the woodland floor.

Indian Paintbrush

other names: Desert Paintbrush
height: 6" to 18"
season: March to October

Look carefully for the narrow pale-green flowers hidden amongst the bright red, orange, or yellow bracts. The roots of a paintbrush can burrow into the roots of a different plant, such as sagebrush, and then steal part of its food. Because of that ability, paintbrush is called a root parasite.

Magenta Four O'Clock

other names: Desert Four
O'Clock, Maravilla
height: up to 18"
season: April to September

Look for mounds of these night-blooming flowers to open about four o'clock each afternoon. The showy blossoms have no petals; the magenta color is on the sepals. Given lots of moisture, the blossoms get so abundant they nearly hide the deep-green, heart-shaped leaves.

Castilleja spp.

Mirabilis multiflora

Calochortus ambiguus

9

Desert Scrub

Prickly mesquite, palo verde, and ironwood are associated with the desert scrub life zone. This zone has the most diverse cactus species. Many wildflowers here are annuals, which means the plant must grow from a seed each year. Sit very still to spot a pocket mouse or kangaroo rat, and listen for black-throated sparrows and cactus wrens. In warm weather, always be on the lookout for shy rattlesnakes—they don't like to be surprised.

Mexican Poppy

other names: Gold Poppy
height: 6" to 12"
season: February to April

Mexicans call this "poppy of the countryside," because it grows in thick patches. Leaves are a lacy, gray-green color, and blossoms close at night or on cloudy days, and stretch open to greet the sun.

Heronsbill

other names: Filaree, Clocks,
    Redstem Heronsbill
height: 6" to12"
season: February to June

This plant gets its name from the long, skinny seedpods that stick straight up. After the seeds mature, the seedpod falls to the ground and twists into a corkscrewlike spiral, awaiting a good rainfall. When the pod gets wet it uncoils and pushes the seed into the ground.

Bladderpod

other names: Gordon's
    Bladderpod, Beadpod
height: 6" to 8", often lying
    along the ground
season: February to April

Look for this among the first blossoms of springtime. The fruits are puffy, beadlike shapes, and livestock enjoy munching them.

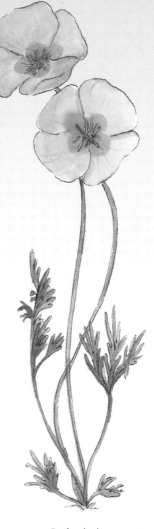

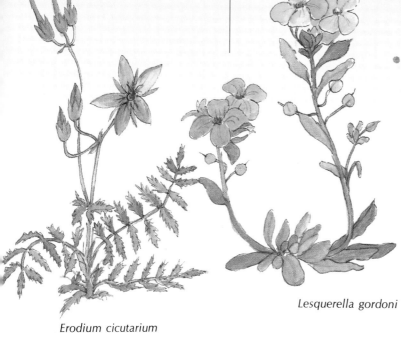

Lesquerella gordoni

Erodium cicutarium

Eschscholzia mexicana

Yucca

other names: Soaptree Yucca, Palmila
height: up to 5'
season: May to July

Skewerlike leaves have hairy fibers along their edges, and cream-colored blossoms shoot up high above the leaf-clump. Indians used every part of this plant. They twisted the tough fibers into rope to make sandals and baskets, used the roots as a soap, and ate the buds, flowers, and young stalks.

Yucca baccata

Brittlebush

other names: Incienso
height: 2' to 3'
season: March to May

Showy flowers cover this shrub and hide the brittle branches. Its sticky resin was burned as incense by early Catholic priests, and Indians like to chew it as gum.

Encelia farinosa

Ajo Lily

other names: Desert Lily
height: 6" to 12"
season: February to April

"Ajo" (AH-hoe) is Spanish for garlic, and the garlicky-tasting bulbs of this lily are edible. But you would have to dig down about two feet in the hard desert soil to find them. It's far better to just enjoy the blossom, which looks a lot like an Easter lily.

Hesperocallis undulata

Arizona Poppy

other names: Desert Poppy,
    Summer Poppy
height: 12" to 18"
season: July to September

This isn't really a poppy, but it looks like one. And just like poppies, it often covers a hillside with brilliant color. The blossom has five orange petals and a crimson center.

Kallstroemia grandiflora

Sand Verbena

other names: none
height: 10" high, with stems
    up to 3' long
season: February to May

That sweet-smelling pink and lavender carpet covering miles of sandy soils and dunes after winter rains is probably sand verbena. The flower head is composed of tiny individual flowers, each with a white center and wavy edges.

Abronia villosa

Desert Globemallow

other names: Desert Hollyhock, Apricot Mallow,
    Sore-eye Poppy
height: 18'' to 3'
season: February to May

Blossoms are usually apricot-colored, but can range from whitish to red. Tiny starburstlike hairs cover the leaves, which have varying shapes. A single globemallow root can send out up to a hundred flowering stems.

Sphaeralcea ambigua

Desert Marigold

other names: none
height: 12''
season: March to October

The name marigold honors the Virgin Mary— "Mary's Gold." This plant blooms for a long time, and the outer rays often bleach out and look papery.

Baileya multiradiata

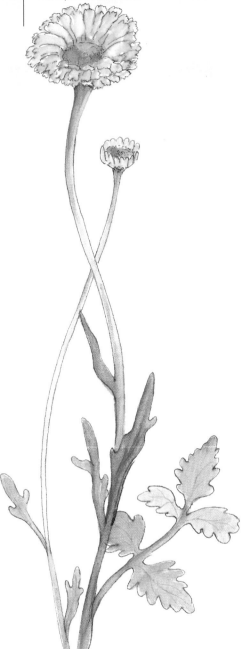

13

Cactus

Arizona has more than seventy species of cactus, some of which grow nowhere else on earth. Some are only two inches tall, while the giant saguaro grows as tall as fifty feet—that's as high as a five-story building!

A cactus sends down a taproot to anchor itself in the ground. Shallow roots spread around the taproot like an umbrella. These roots suck up moisture from rain showers. Cacti change water into a thick substance which does not evaporate quickly, and store it in expandable tissues. When plenty of rain falls, many cacti swell up with the feast and then very slowly use the stored water to help them through dry spells. Some cacti survive on stored fluids for several years.

Spines on cacti grow in bunches from common centers, called areoles. Thick, waxy skin hinders evaporation of fluids, and food is manufactured by the outer green cells of the stems.

Cacti produce beautiful, brightly colored blossoms that may last only a day. It's often startling to see an exquisite blossom nestled amongst stern, forbidding spines.

Pincushion

other names: Fishhook
height: 6" to 10"
season: April to June

This low-growing cactus is easy to overlook until springtime, when lavender or pink blossoms form a beautiful crown atop the stems. The stems have many long, curved spines, and the cactus looks like a pincushion full of fishhooks. Don't let it catch you!

Mammillaria microcarpa

Grizzly Bear

other names: Old Man Prickly
Pear
height: 12" to 18"
season: May to June

Real grizzly bears have long, white-tipped hairs, and like that great bear this cactus is covered with long, flexible, whitish spines. Grizzly bear cactus grow in large clumps, and produce either red or yellow flowers.

Opuntia erinaces var. ursina

Fishhook Barrel

other names: Compass Cactus
height: 2' to 8'
season: July to September

"Fero" means fierce, and the hooked spines are indeed fierce. This is the tallest barrel cactus in Arizona. Cells grow faster on the shaded north side, so this cactus often "points" to the sunny south, hence the name compass cactus. Barrel cacti are used to make cactus candy.

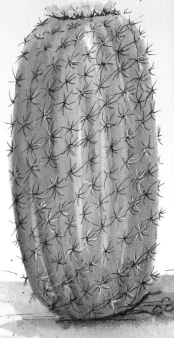

Ferocactus wislizenii

Rainbow Cactus

other names: none
height: 6" to 12"
season: June to August

Closely clustered spines grow in bands of alternating red and white to give this cactus a rainbow appearance. The pink, lavender or yellow flowers look too big for the stem, and often grow in a circle to form a cactus crown.

Echinocereus pectinatus

Beavertail

other names: Prickly Pear
height: 12"
season: March to April

Vivid rose-colored flowers nearly cover the beavertail in springtime. This prickly pear is easy to identify because it has no long spines. Instead, "glochids" (strongly barbed bristles) grow in clumps on the stem. Each stem is rounded and flat, like a beaver's tail.

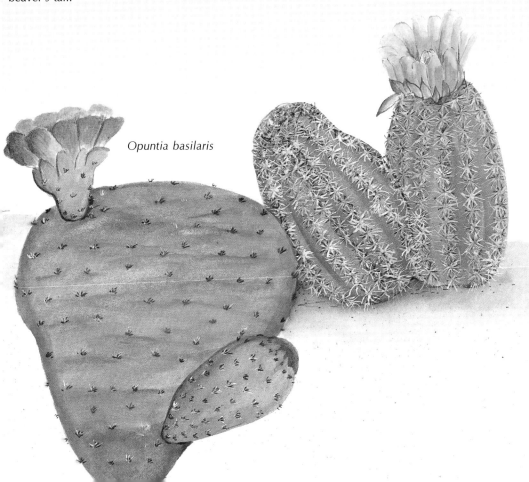

Opuntia basilaris

Saguaro

other names: Giant Cactus
height: up to 50'
season: May to June

The saguaro (sah-WAH-row) is the largest cactus in the United States. It can live 200 years and weigh as much as twelve tons. Saguaro's night-blooming blossom is the state flower of Arizona. The fruit bursts open in July, displaying a ruby-red lining and abundant seeds. Tiny elf owls make cozy nests out of old woodpecker holes in the thorny stems of saguaros.

Organ Pipe

other names: Pitahaya
height: 5' to 25'
season: May to June

The tall, upright stems resemble the sound pipes for an organ. Each stem produces night-blooming flowers and delicious red fruits prized by the Papago Indians. Organ Pipe Cactus National Monument was established to protect these cacti.

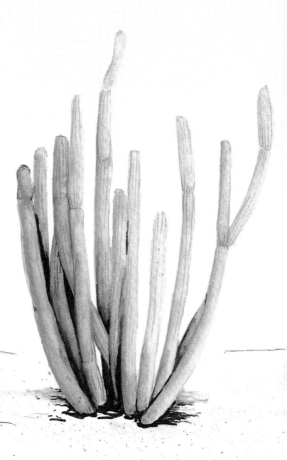

Carnegiea gigantea

Stenocereus thurberi

Teddy Bear Cholla

other names: none
height: 2' to 5'
season: February to April

Don't cuddle this teddy bear! Although it looks soft and fuzzy, tiny barbs on the end of each spine stick in your skin at the slightest touch. New plants form when joints from the plant drop onto the ground and take root. The inconspicuous flowers are greenish-yellow, often streaked with lavender.

Prickly Pear

other names: Tuna Cactus, Engelmann
    Prickly pear
height: up to 5' high, with clumps 10'
    in diameter
season: April to June

Prickly pear is the most abundant and widely distributed cactus in Arizona. Its tasty fruit, called a "tuna," is a burgundy-colored, juicy, pear-shaped treat enjoyed by both humans and animals. Be sure to peel off the minuscule spines, called glochids, before eating the fruit.

Opuntia phaeacantha

Opuntia bigelovii

Douglas-fir Forest

Douglas-fir remind us of Christmas trees. They make thick forests, often mixed with white firs and quaking aspens.

The White Mountains and the North Rim of the Grand Canyon have large Douglas-fir forests. Wildflowers often grow in the clearings between these big evergreens. Watch for deer, porcupines, and maybe even bears.

Canada Violet

other names: Violet
height: 12″
season: April to August

The only violet color on these violets is in the tiny veins, and in a hint of color on the back. The lower, larger flower petal forms a landing platform for bees. Violets are edible—the leaves have lots of vitamins A and C, and the blossoms are sometimes used to make candy, jelly, and syrup.

Strawberry

other names: none
height: 4″
season: May to October

Make a note when you see the pretty white, five-petaled blossom, so you can return later to savor the sweet wild strawberry. Yum!

Fragaria ovalis

Monkshood

other names: Friar's Cap,
    Blue Weed
height: 2′ to 6′
season: June to September

The upper sepal of this deep violet-blue flower forms an arching hood, like the hood of a monk's habit. Peek under the hood to find the monk's "face," composed of two petals and the stamen and pistil. We get heart medicine from some species of monkshood.

Aconitum columbianum

Viola canadensis

Cutleaf Coneflower

other names: Goldenglow
height: 3' to 6'
season: July to September

The center cone of disk flowers juts up from the drooping yellow rays. Leaves have deeply cut, toothed edges. Coneflowers are mildly poisonous to cattle.

Wheeler Thistle

other names: none
height: 2' to 3'
season: June to October

Pale lavender flowers adorn a stem bearing numerous spiny leaves. Thistle seeds ride the wind on feathery little parachutes, and often inhabit areas where the ground has been disturbed. Most thistles are edible and have medicinal uses.

Rudbeckia laciniata

Cirsium wheeleri

19

Spruce-fir Forest

The spruce-fir life zone is found on the highest plateaus and mountains. Here, wildflowers seek the sunniest spots, and often have wet feet from snow melt. In late summer you can munch on delicious blueberries and currants while keeping an eye out for bright wildflowers. Red squirrels may chatter at you, and blue grouse, nutcrackers, grosbeaks, finches, and sparrows will serenade you.

Gentian

other names: Pleated Gentian
height: 12''
season: August to October

The deep blue, funnel-shaped gentian blossoms only open when the sun shines. Navajo Indians used this plant to treat headaches.

Marsh Marigold

other names: Elk's Lip, King's Cup
height: 1'' to 8''
season: June to September

These water-loving plants grow in boggy areas. The stems and undersides of the leaves are tinged with purple, and the pretty white blossoms have bright yellow anthers in their centers.

Caltha leptosepala

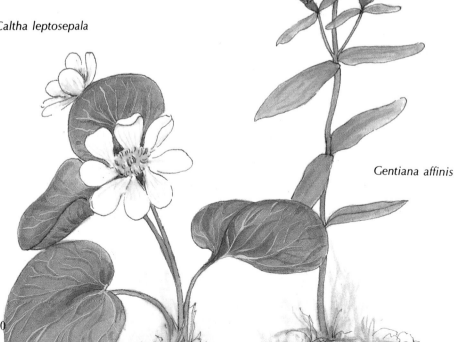

Gentiana affinis

Harebell

other names: Bellflower, Bluebell
height: 6'' to 12''
season: July to September

Campanula is Latin for "little bell," and these lovely blue bell-shaped blossoms nod gently atop their slender stems. Navajo and Zuni indians used the roots to make some medicines.

Campanula parryi

Fairy Slipper

other names: Calypso Orchid,
　　　　　　Venus-slipper
height: up to 8''
season: June to July

This ornate and exotic flower is found in the deep shade of the forest. The pink or purple blossom is streaked or spotted with brownish-purple. Calypso was a shy sea nymph. Perhaps she wore these flowers as slippers? They have a sweet, subtle aroma, so take time to smell them.

Calypso bulbosa

Orange agoseris

other names: Burnt-orange
　　　　　　Dandelion
height: 4'' to 12''
season: June to August

The dark orange flower head looks a bit like a dandelion, but the agoseris' rays are spaced farther apart and turn purplish as they age. The seeds are carried far and wide by silvery umbrellalike bristles.

Agoseria aurantiaca

Baneberry

other names: none
height: 2' to 3'
season: May to October

Short fuzzy clusters of white flowers are followed by oval white berries with a dark spot on the end. These poisonous berries gradually turn red.

Checkermallow

other names: New Mexico
    Checkermallow, Canyon
    Hollyhock
height: 1' to 3'
season: June to September

The mallow family has many important plants, such as cotton and okra. Next time you toast a marshmallow over a campfire, think about these flowers—marshmallows were originally flavored with a European species of mallow.

Bluebells

other names: Franciscan bluebells
height: 12" to 24"
season: June to September

Clusters of tiny blue blossoms weigh down the tops of each plant. Bluebells often have pink or white tinges of color in young blossoms.

Mertensia franciscana

Sidalcea neomexicana

Actaea arguta

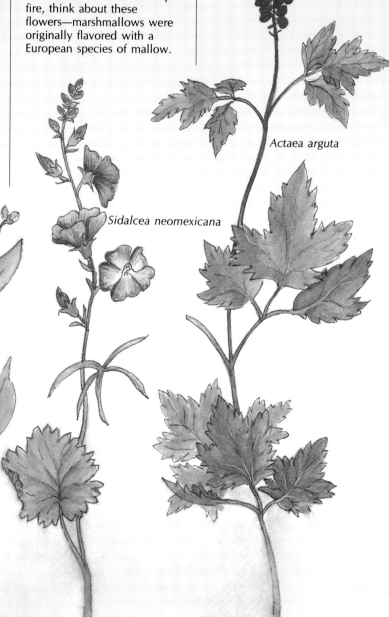

Corn Lily

other names: False Hellebore
height: 4' to 6'
season: July to August

From a distance the tall stalk and deeply veined leaves of this plant make it look like garden corn. But don't sample any—corn lily is so poisonous it can even kill honeybees.

Rocky Mountain Pussytoes

other names: none
height: 2'' to 6''
season: May to August

Like furry little toes on a kitten, pussytoes invite you to gently touch them. The tiny flowers are hidden within the white, furry "toes," or bracts. Early Navajo Indians smoked the leaves of this plant when praying for rain.

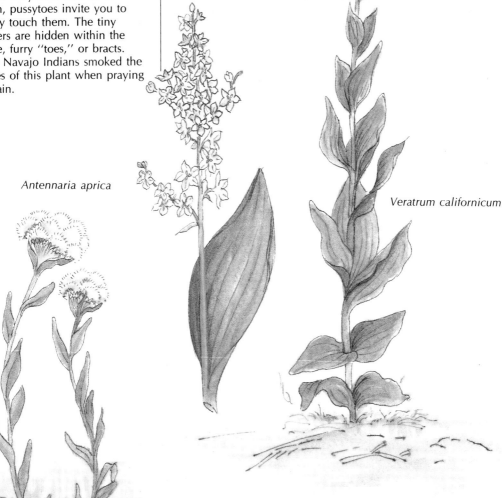

Antennaria aprica

Veratrum californicum

Ponderosa Pine Forest

The ponderosa pine is a tall, straight tree with reddish-brown, grooved bark. The long needles grow in clusters and let sunlight filter through to the grassy forest floor. Ponderosa pine forests cover most of the Kaibab Plateau and Mogollon Rim. Keep your eyes open for deer, squirrels, rabbits, chickadees, and green treefrogs.

Mullein

other names: Flannel Mullein, Velvet Plant,
   Woolly Mullein
height: 2' to 7'
season: June to August

Yellow blossoms cluster around the top of mullein's tall spike, and starburst-shaped hairs grow so densely that the whole plant appears woolly. Ancient Romans and Greeks dipped the tall stalks in tallow to make torches.

Verbascum thapsus

Arizona Wild Rose

other names: none
height: 3' to 4'
season: May to July

Sweet-smelling pink flowers adorn a thorny stem. Birds, people, and animals eat the fruits, or ''rosehips,'' which have lots of vitamin C. Giving someone a rose means you love them.

Rosa arizonica

Skyrocket

other names: Desert Trumpet,
    Skunk Flower, Fairy
    Trumpet
height: 1' to 3'
season: May to September

The blossom's long crimson-red tube flares out into a starburst, like skyrocketing fireworks. Hummingbirds love to sample its sweet nectar. Another of its common names comes from the skunk-like odor of its leaves.

Lupine

other names: Palmer Lupine,
    Sundial Plant
height: 12'' to 24''
season: April to October

This is the most common lupine in ponderosa pine forests. Lupines are part of the pea family, and enrich the soil they live in. It is also called a sundial plant because its leaves may follow the sun across the sky, then fold at night.

Yarrow

other names: Milfoil, Plumajillo.
height: 12'' to 24''
season: June to September

Plumajillo is Spanish for "little feather," and the feathery, fernlike leaves make this plant easy to identify. Yarrow is very aromatic and has many medicinal uses.

Achillea lanulosa

Lupinus palmeri

Ipomopsis aggregata

25

Blue Flag

other names: Rocky Mountain Iris
height: 8" to 20"
season: May to June

Iris is the Greek word for "rainbow," referring to this plant's multicolored blossom. Irises have many traditional medicinal uses, and the silky leaf fibers were used to make twine and rope for fishing and hunting.

Columbine

other names: Golden Columbine,
    Yellow Columbine
height: 1' to 4'
season: April to September

Aquilla is Latin for "eagle," because the spurs on this blossom are like an eagle's talons. Most columbines in Arizona are yellow, but maybe you'll see some that are blue or violet or red.

Iris missouriensis

Aquilegia chrysantha

Sneezeweed

other names: Owlclaws
height: 2' to 4'
season: June to September

Aaaachoo! Some people sneeze after smelling this flower. The long droopy rays surround a disk of tiny golden flowers. The plant has some medicinal uses, and Navajo Indians made chewing gum from the roots.

Helenium hoopesii

Purple Vetch

other names: American Vetch
height: 2' to 4'
season: May to September

Slender tendrils coil around other plants and allow purple vetch to climb upward. The seeds and leaves are eaten by many birds, such as grouse, mourning doves, and pheasants.

Vicia americana

Shooting Star

other names: Peacock Flower,
    Bird's Bill, Sailor Cap,
    Mosquito Bill
height: 4'' to 24''
season: April to August

There are approximately ten species of shooting stars in the West. Flower color ranges from white to pink to deep purple. They all share the appearance of being inside out—that is, of "shooting" downward. Native Americans roasted and ate the roots and leaves.

Dodecatheon pulchellum

27

Conclusion

"Over here! Look at me!" shout the bright colors of a wildflower. The showy blossoms attract us, but more importantly, attract insects and other flying and crawling visitors who pollinate each flower. Bees, moths, beetles, butterflies, hummingbirds, even ants and bats are essential for the wildflowers to make seeds. So when you bend down to enjoy the sweet smell of a fresh blossom, remember to share the space with other creatures. Wildflowers may like us to look at them, but they depend on their other visitors for survival.

. . . Little flower—but if I could understand
What you are, root and all, and all in all,
I should know what God and man is.

Lord Tennyson

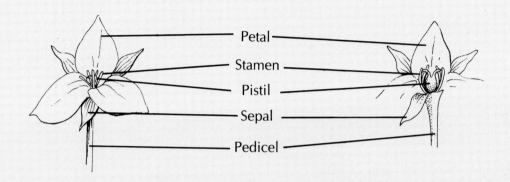

Petal

Stamen

Pistil

Sepal

Pedicel

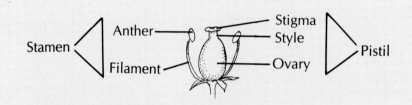

Stamen

Anther

Filament

Stigma

Style

Ovary

Pistil

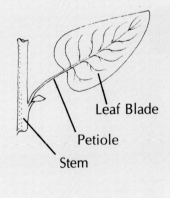

Leaf Blade

Petiole

Stem

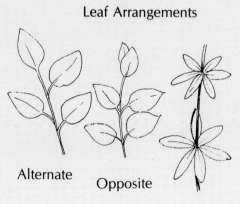

Leaf Arrangements

Alternate   Opposite

Whorl

Alpine	Pertaining to or inhabiting mountains.
Alternate	Not opposite each other.
Annual	A plant that lives for one season.
Anther	The part of the stamen containing pollen.
Berry	A fleshy fruit containing seeds.
Biennial	A plant that lives for two years.
Bulb	A plant bud usually below the ground.
Corm	A bulb-like underground swelling of a stem.
Composite	Flower heads composed of clusters of ray and disk flowers.
Disk flower	The tubular flowers in the center part of a composite flower head.
Evergreen	Bearing green leaves throughout the year.
Filament	The stalk of the stamen.
Flower head	A dense cluster of flowers atop a stem.
Fruit	Seed-bearing part of a plant; ripened ovary.
Fungus	A plant lacking chlorophyll which reproduces by spores.
Gland	A spot or area that produces a sticky substance.
Habitat	The community where a plant naturally grows and lives.
Head	A dense cluster of flowers atop a stem.
Herb	A plant with no woody stem above ground.
Hybrid	A cross between two species.
Irregular	Nonsymmetrical in shape.
Nectar	A sweet liquid produced by flowers that attracts insects.
Opposite	Pairs of leaves opposite each other on a stem.
Ovary	Part of the pistil which contains the developing seeds.
Parasitic	Growing on and deriving nourishment from another plant.
Pedicel	The supporting stem of a single flower.
Perennial	A plant that lives from year to year.
Petals	The floral leaves inside the sepals which attract pollinators.
Petiole	The stem supporting a leaf.
Pistil	The seed-bearing organ of a flower.
Pollen	Powder-like cells produced by stamens.
Ray flower	The flowers around the edge of a flower head; each flower may resemble a single petal.
Regular	Alike in size and shape.
Rhizome	An underground stem or rootstock.
Saprophyte	A plant that lives on dead organic matter.
Sepal	Outermost floral leaf which protects the delicate petals.
Spur	A hollow appendage of a petal or sepal.
Stamen	The pollen producing organ of a flower.
Stigma	The end of the pistil that collects pollen.
Style	The slender stalk of a pistil.
Succulent	Pulpy, soft, and juicy.
Tendril	A slender twining extension of a leaf or stem.
Tuber	A thickened underground stem, having numerous buds.
Whorl	Three or more leaves or branches growing from a common point.

Where to See Wildflowers

Wildflowers can be found anywhere in Arizona, but some of the best places are state and federal parks, forests, recreation areas, and monuments. Many of these areas have campgrounds, picnic areas, nature trails, and interpretive services to help visitors see and appreciate these lands and their wildflowers. You can get information about these areas by contacting the following organizations:

Apache-Sitgreaves National Forest
Coconino National Forest
Tonto National Forest
Prescott National Forest
Kaibab National Forest
Northern Arizona Natural History
   Association
P.O. Box 1633
Flagstaff, AZ 86002
(602) 646-6853

Imperial National Wildlife Refuge
Kaibab National Forest
Coronado National Forest
Tonto National Forest
Southwest Natural and Cultural Heritage
   Association
Drawer E
Albuquerque, NM 87103
(602) 622-1999

Arizona-Sonora Desert Museum
Arizona-Sonora Desert Museum
2021 N. Kinney Rd.
Tucson, AZ 85743
(602) 883-1380

Desert Botanical Garden
Desert Botanical Garden
1201 N. Galvin Parkway
Phoenix, AZ 85008
(602) 941-1225

Grand Canyon National Park
Grand Canyon Natural History
   Association
P.O. Box 399
Grand Canyon, AZ 86023
(602) 638-2481

Painted Desert
Petrified Forest National Park
Petrified Forest Museum Association
P.O. Box 2277
Petrified Forest, AZ 86028
(602) 524-6228

Glen Canyon National Recreation
   Area
Glen Canyon Natural History
   Association
P.O. Box 581
Page, AZ 86040
(602) 645-3532

Other outstanding wildflower sites in
   Arizona:
Canyon de Chelly National Monument
Chiricahua National Monument
Cibola National Wildlife Refuge
Havasu National Wildlife Refuge
Lake Havasu State Park
Organ Pipe Cactus National
   Monument
Painted Rocks State Park
Picacho Peak State Park
Saguaro National Monument
Sunset Crater National Monument
Tonto National Monument
Walnut Canyon National Monument
Wupatki National Monument